P9-DDF-661

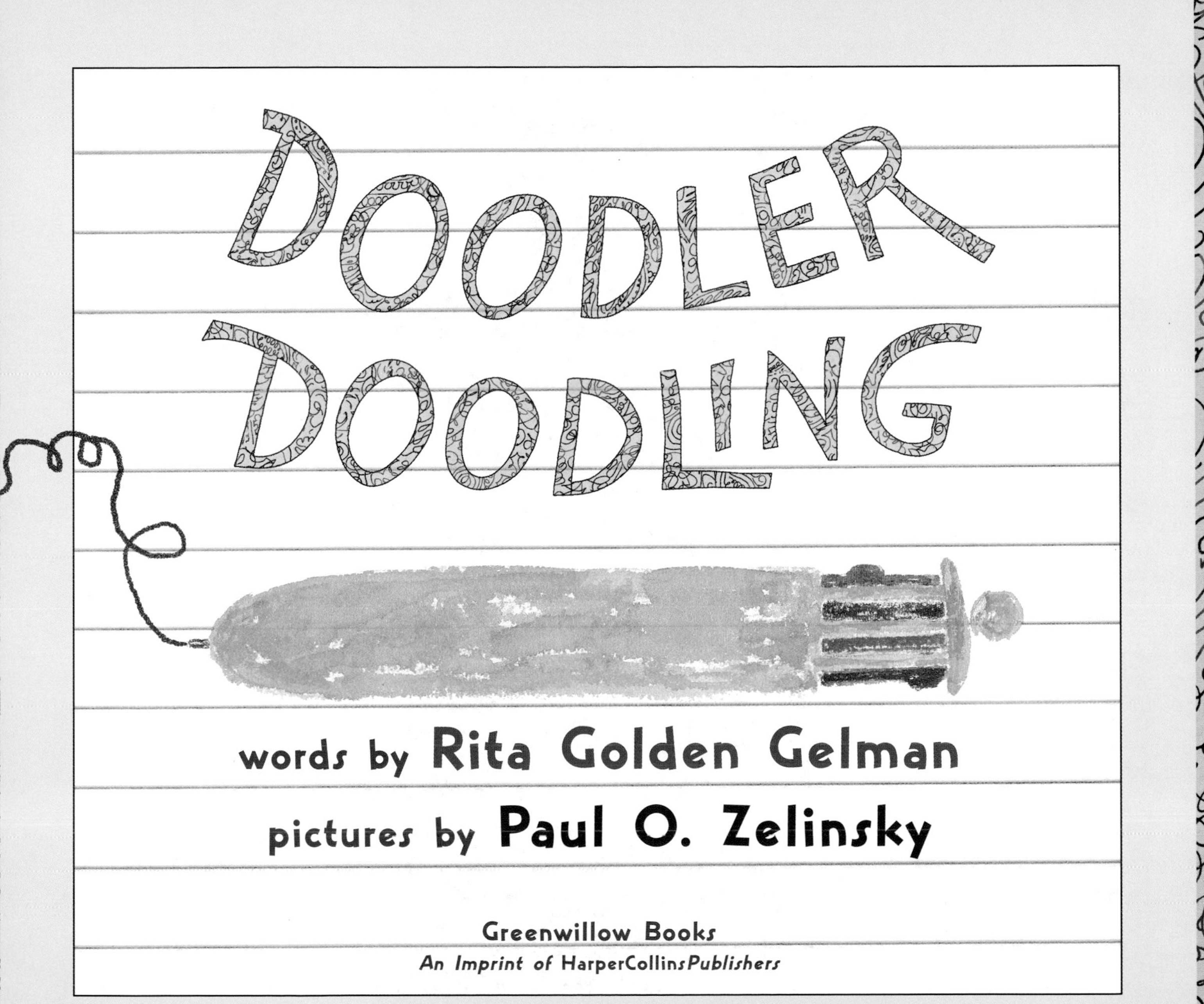

DOODLER DOODLING

words by Rita Golden Gelman

pictures by Paul O. Zelinsky

Greenwillow Books

An Imprint of HarperCollinsPublishers

Doodler Doodling
Text copyright © 2004 by Rita Golden Gelman
Illustrations copyright © 2004 by Paul O. Zelinsky
All rights reserved.
Manufactured in China by South China Printing Company Ltd.
www.harperchildrens.com

The art for DOODLER DOODLING was drawn in bits and pieces using watercolor and black pen, then scanned and manipulated in the computer to arrive at the finished images.
The text type is Circus Mouse Book-Medium.

Library of Congress Cataloging-in-Publication Data
Gelman, Rita Golden.
Doodler doodling / words by Rita Golden Gelman ; pictures by Paul O. Zelinsky.
p. cm.
"Greenwillow Books."
Summary: Teachers teach, fliers fly, painters paint, climbers climb—and teachers fly, climbers paint. . . .
ISBN 0-688-16645-8 (trade).
I. Zelinsky, Paul O., ill. II. Title.
PZ7.G2837 Do 2003 [E]—dc21 2002935326

First Edition 10 9 8 7 6 5 4 3 2 1

Greenwillow Books

With love to all my friends at
Vivekanand Camp II,
New Delhi, India, where people
are always people-ing
—R. G. G.

In memory of warm
and silky Skimby
—P. O. Z.

Teachers teaching.

Fliers flying.

Fliers teaching.

Teachers flying.

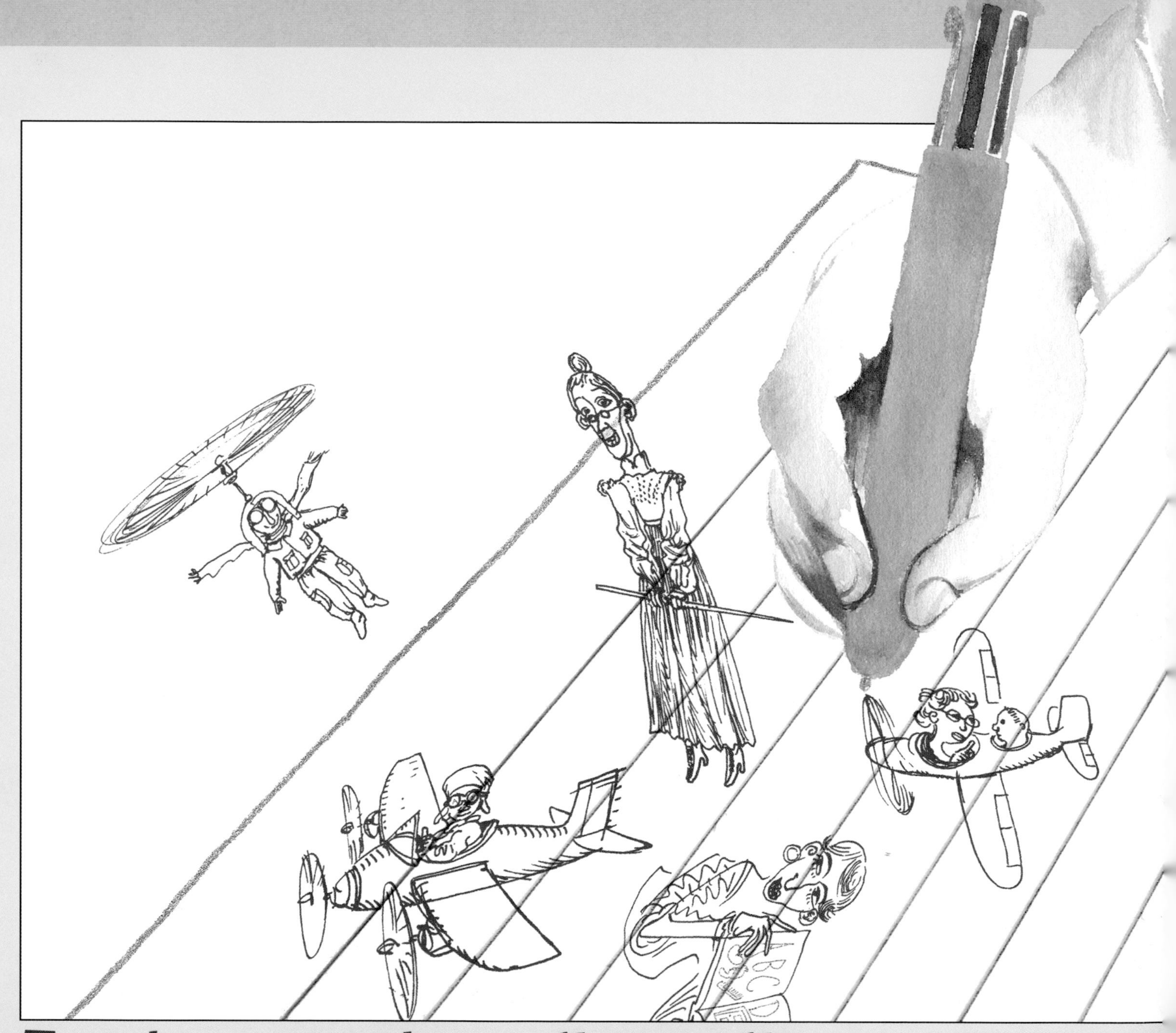

Teachers teaching flying fliers.

Fliers flying teachers.

What?

Painters painting.

Climbers climbing.

Climbers painting. Painters climbing.

Painters painting climbing climbers.

Climbers climbing painters.
Whee!

Fliers flying teachers teaching painters painting climbers.

Throwers throwing. Huggers hugging.

Huggers throwing. Throwers hugging.

Huggers hugging throwing throwers.

Throwers throwing huggers.

No!

Bakers baking. Mowers mowing.

Mowers baking.

throwers painting huggers mowing

Bakers mowing.

Bakers baking mowing mowers.

Mowers mowing bakers.

Painters hugging bakers climbing

Stop!

wers baking teachers teaching.

fliers throwing climbers flying mov

WOW!